Anthony and Sabrina

by Ray Prather

Macmillan Publishing Co., Inc.
New York
Collier Macmillan Publishers
London

Macmillan Publishing Co., Inc., 866 Third Avenue, New York, N.Y. 10022
Collier-Macmillan Canada Ltd., Toronto, Ontario
Library of Congress catalog card number: 73–3888
Printed in the United States of America
10 9 8 7 6 5 4 3 2 1

The three-color illustrations were prepared as black pencil-and-wash drawings with
overlays for yellow and brown. The typeface is Alphatype Bookman, with the display set in
Cooper Black Italic.

Library of Congress Cataloging in Publication Data   Prather, Ray.   Anthony and Sabrina.
[1. Brothers and sisters—Fiction.   2. Farm life—Florida]   I. Title.   PZ7.P887An
[E]   73–3888   ISBN 0-02-775030-2

For Raymond Prather, Sr.–Dad

"Whew, sure is hot."

"Yeah. Sure is."

"What're we going to do today, Anthony?"

"I don't know."

"What did we do yesterday, Anthony?"

"I don't remember."

"Well, why don't you remember, Anthony?"

"Girl, who do you think I am, Superman? Now get up and catch."

"Hey, Anthony, let's ask Mother to take us over to Big Ma's."

"Well, go ask her."

"Why do I always have to ask?"

"Because it was your idea, Sabrina."

"But I asked last time."

"No, you didn't."

"Yes, I did."

"No, you didn't."

"Yes, I did."

"Oh, all right, Sabrina. I'll ask."

"Mother, will you take Sabrina and me to Big Ma's?"

"Yes, but you'll have to wait until I finish washing."

"I'm sitting in front, Anthony."

"No, I am. I asked her, didn't I?"

"So what?"

"Stop that fussing, both of you, and go clean up your rooms."

"Yes, Ma'am."

"Yes'm."

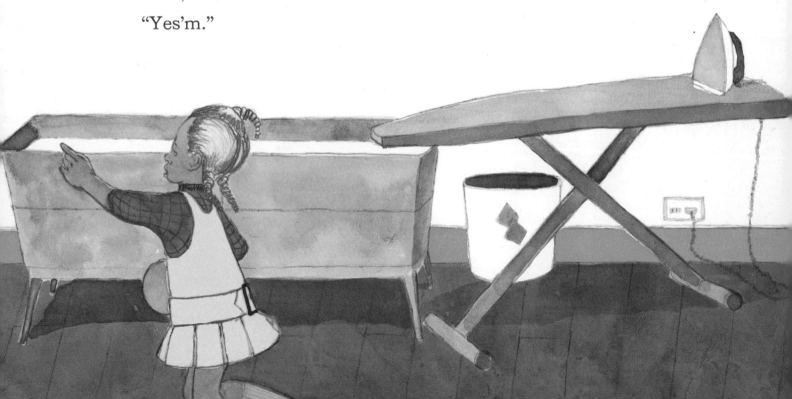

"Sure wish I could wear my new dress that Daddy bought me."

"Well, why don't you?"

"Maybe I will."

"Well, what are you waiting for?"

"For you to shut up."

"Girl, one of these days I'm going to fix you good,
  you hear? Now, get out of my room. I'm dressing."

"Anthony, did you straighten up your room?"

"Yes'm."

"Sabrina, did you put that dirty dress in the hamper?"

"Yes, Ma'am."

"Hey, Sabrina. I thought you were going to wear your new dress."

"Ah, shut up, Anthony, and hold the door."

"Girl, don't you tell me what to do."

"All right, you two. Get in the car and let's go."

"Pssst. Anthony, ask Mother to drive faster."

"You do it. It's your turn."

"Hey, Big Ma. Hey, Big Pa. How're you doing?"

"Sorta tolerable, I guess. And how's my babies?"

"Oh, we're doing fine. We came to play and Mother,
 she came to talk."

"Come on, Sabrina, let's go get on the swing."

"I'm first, Anthony."

"Okay. You're first."

"Sabrina, let's slip off and go see the pigs."

"Okay."

"And don't you go and tell like you did last time. You hear, girl?"

"Well, it was your fault I tore my dress."

"I didn't tell you to climb that barbed-wire fence."

"But you climbed it, Anthony."

"Yeah, but I still didn't make you. Anyway, stop fussing
  and get down and come on."

"Will you carry me on your back, Anthony?"

"Huh. If I'm a mule I will."

"Look at that one, Sabrina. He's kind of fat and ugly, isn't he?"

"Yeah, he looks just like you."

"Sabrina, you're asking for it. You do that one more time and I'll…."

"Oh, Anthony—I smell plums, don't you?"

"Yeah, but I didn't forget what you said."

"I'll race you to the tree. Last one there is a muddy pig."

"Anthony, I'll bet there're a lot of snakes out here, huh?"

"Ah, girl, ain't no snakes out here."

"What's that I hear then, Anthony?"

"Nothing but your ears. Shut up and eat your plums."

"I don't want any more."

"Let's go ride the mule."

"No."

"Let's milk the cow."

"No."

"Want to go climb the persimmon tree, Sabrina?"

"No, it's too high."

"Want to go chase the chickens?"

"No."

"Let's go wade in the pond."

"Okay."

"Take off your shoes."

"Watch out. I'm coming in."

"You better be careful, girl. It's slippery out here."

"So?"

SPLASH!

"Look at you. I told you to be careful."

"But, Anthony . . . ."

"You're always getting me in trouble."

"Yeah, but . . . ."

"But nothing. It was all your fault. Get up. I'm going to make
    you climb that persimmon tree anyway. And you're going to stay
    up there until you're dry. And you'd better not tell, either."

"But, Anthony . . . ."

"And shut up. Haven't you done enough?"

"Anthony."

"Yeah."

"I'm dry. May I come down now?"

"Yeah."

"Will you catch me, Anthony?"

"No. Climb down yourself. And let's go back to the house."

"Well, what have my two sweet babies been doing today?"

"Hee, hee, hee, just playing."

"Well, Anthony...he...ouch...yeah,
 Big Ma, we were just playing."

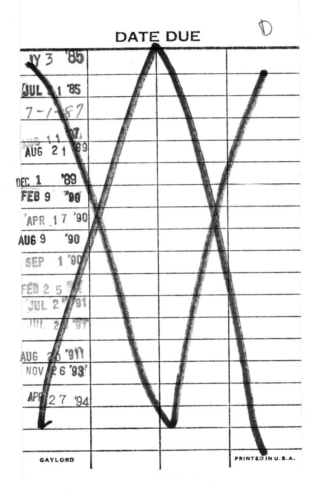

DATE DUE